Sleep, Black Bear, Sleep

By **Jane Yolen** and **Heidi E. Y. Stemple**

Illustrated by **Brooke Dyer**

SCHOLASTIC INC.

New York Toronto London Auckland Sydney
Mexico City New Delhi Hong Kong Buenos Aires

ISBN-13: 978-0-545-11353-3
ISBN-10: 0-545-11353-9

Text copyright © 2007 by Jane Yolen and Heidi E. Y. Stemple. Illustrations copyright © 2007 by Brooke Dyer.
All rights reserved. Published by Scholastic Inc., 557 Broadway, New York, NY 10012, by arrangement with HarperCollins Children's Books, a division of HarperCollins Publishers. SCHOLASTIC and associated logos are trademarks and/or registered trademarks of Scholastic Inc.

12 11 10 9 8 7 6 5 4 3 2 1   8 9 10 11 12 13/0

Printed in the U.S.A.   40

First Scholastic printing, November 2008

Typography by Carla Weise

Sleep, little Caroline, sleep.
Sleep, little Amelia, sleep.
—J.Y.

To Maddison and Glendon—
for all the nights I rocked you to sleep
and all the nights I didn't get to.
—H.E.Y.S.

To my little peanut.
—B.D.

Sleep, little one, sleep.

Your dreams are long and deep.

Sleep in your burrow, cave, or den,

Sleep till the winter's done and then

Rise up and start all over again.
Sleep, little one, sleep.

Sleep, black bear, sleep.
The hills are bare and steep.
You hibernate through winter's snow;
Your heart beats steady, strong, and slow.
You wait till spring to rise and go.
Sleep, black bear, sleep.

Dream, little frog, dream
At the bottom of your stream.
A skim of ice above you high
Is like a graying winter sky.
Don't wake till spring, don't even try.
Dream, little frog, dream.

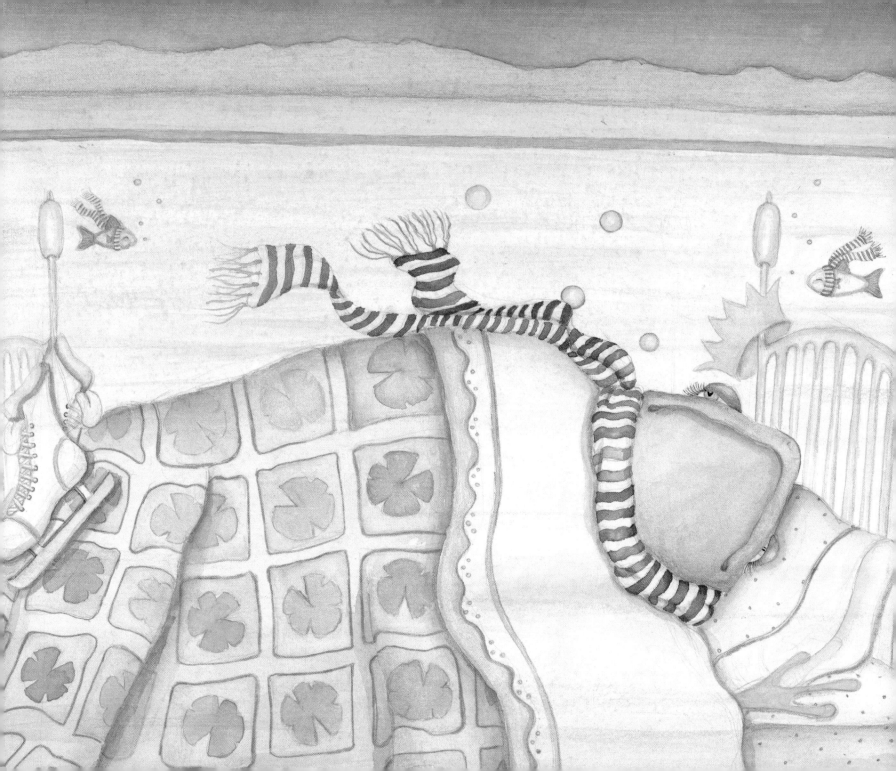

Hang, little bat, hang
With your entire gang.
Tuck your legs and tail in tight
For winter's dark extended night
Until the spring brings warmth and light.
Hang, little bat, hang.

Nap, little snakes, nap,

Heads and tails overlap.

One big tangle keeps you warm

Through nature's cold and winter's storm.

Your breathing takes a slower form.

Nap, little snakes, nap.

Snooze, box turtle, snooze
Within the spot you choose.
Safe from wind and frozen rain
That beats above, a soft refrain,
Till sunlight warms the thawed terrain.
Snooze, box turtle, snooze.

Rest, gopher, rest.
For you the burrow's best.
So find a chamber that will fit,
And settle down inside of it.
And food? Just snack a little bit.
Rest, gopher, rest.

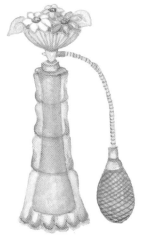

Snore, little skunk, snore,
　Turn over, snore some more.
The winter winds may howl and wail;
Your den is closed with snow and hail.
But you know spring will never fail.
Snore, little skunk, snore.

Nod, badger, nod
Within your house of sod.
Inside your sett you settle down,
Surrounded by familiar ground,
A welcome house in earthy brown.
Nod, badger, nod.

Doze, beaver, doze,

Just let your eyelids close.

When water freezes up your dam,

Too icy for a good tail slam,

Into your lodge you quickly scram.

Doze, beaver, doze.

Hush, little mouse, hush.

This is the final rush.

Do not delay, no time to stall,

Curl up into a little ball

As winter creeps and snowstorms fall.

Hush, little mouse, hush.

Loll, little toad, loll,

Take heed of winter's call.

Dig down and deep within the ooze

As soon as you hear winter's news,

And there prepare a long, cold snooze.

Loll, little toad, loll.

Yawn, chipmunk, yawn
As you cross the lawn.
Duck under rocks and under weeds
To where your winding tunnel leads,
And there amongst your hidden seeds
Yawn, chipmunk, yawn.

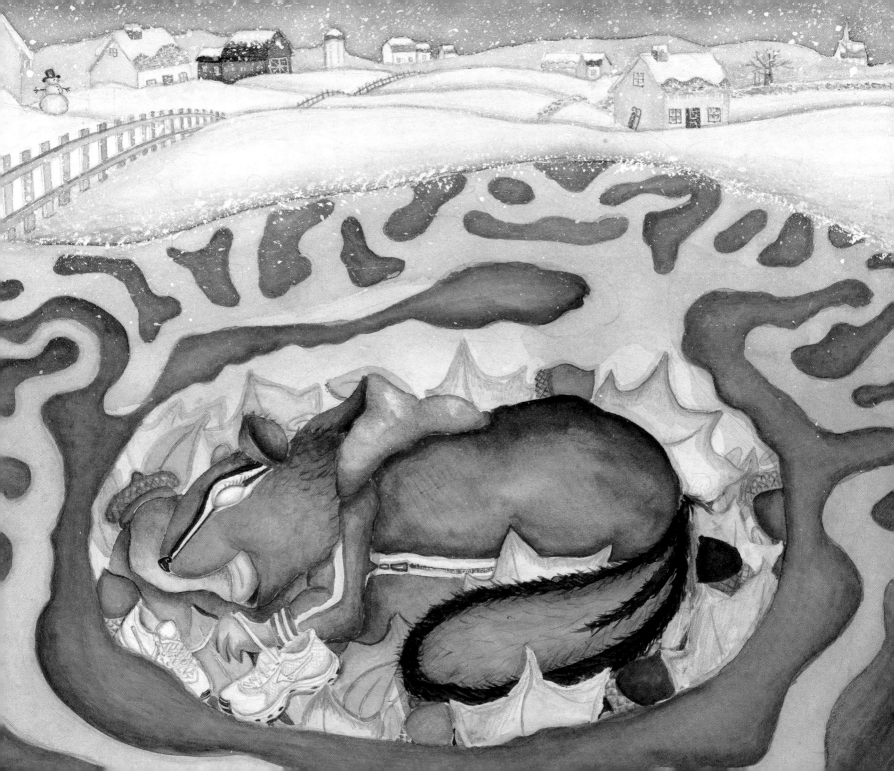

And even YOU, it's time for sleep,

So snuggle down and burrow deep.

The sheet and quilt will keep you warm

Through winter or through summer storm

Till you awaken in the morn.

Sleep, my little child, sleep.